World of Reading

HERA'S PHANTOM FLIGHT

ADAPTED BY ELIZABETH SCHAEFER

BASED ON THE EPISODE "OUT OF DARKNESS," WRITTEN BY KEVIN HOPPS

PRESS
LOS ANGELES • NEW YORK

Printed in the United States of America

First Edition, March 2015 10 9 8 7 6 5 4 3 2 1

Library of Congress Control Number: 2014918866

G658-7729-4-15044

ISBN 978-1-4847-0465-3

Visit the official *Star Wars* website at: www.starwars.com

Meet Hera.

Hera is a very good pilot.

She can fly any ship.

Hera's favorite ship is called the *Ghost*.

Hera and her rebel friends live on board the *Ghost*.

Hera's friends are named Sabine, Chopper, Kanan, Ezra, and Zeb.

The rebels fight against the Empire so that everyone can be free.

Sometimes the Empire's ships try to stop Hera.

But they never win!

Hera also flies the *Phantom*.

The *Phantom* is a much smaller ship than the *Ghost*.

The rebels store the *Phantom* inside the *Ghost*.

Because it is small, the *Phantom* is harder for big ships to see.

The *Phantom* is perfect for secret missions.

Hera is good at finding out secrets.

She learns the Empire's secrets and uses them to plan rebel missions.

On one secret mission, Hera was flying the *Phantom*.

Three TIE fighters spotted her and attacked!

Hera wasn't worried.

Hera dodged their blasts, but she flew too close to a big rock.

The rock scratched the bottom of her ship.

Hera knew right away that the *Phantom* was damaged.

Hera blew up the TIE fighters and flew back into space.

It was time to meet up with the *Ghost*.

Hera docked inside the *Ghost*.

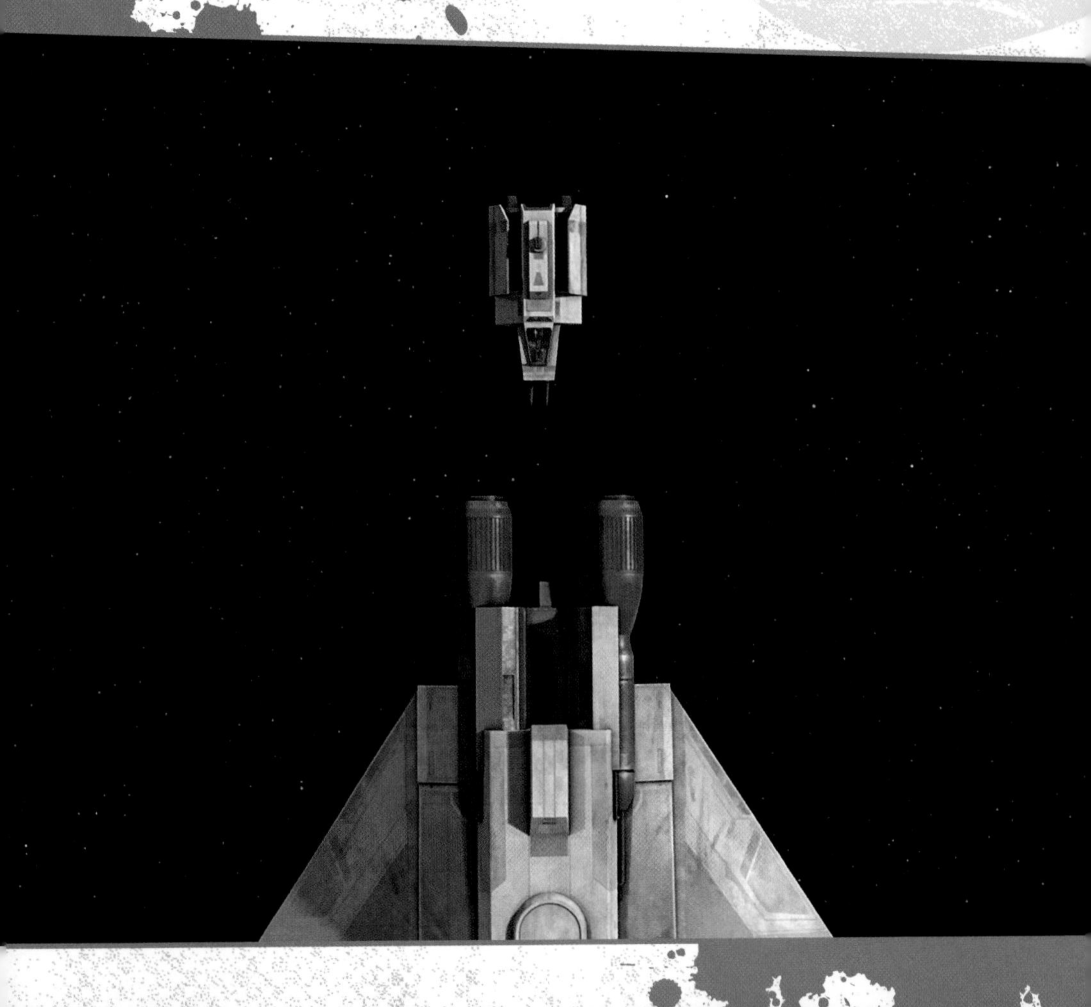

Hera asked Zeb, Ezra, and Chopper to fix the *Phantom*.

But they forgot to.

They were too busy fighting with each other.

The next time Hera flew the *Phantom*, she and Sabine were on a mission to pick up supplies.

Then the *Phantom* started leaking fuel.

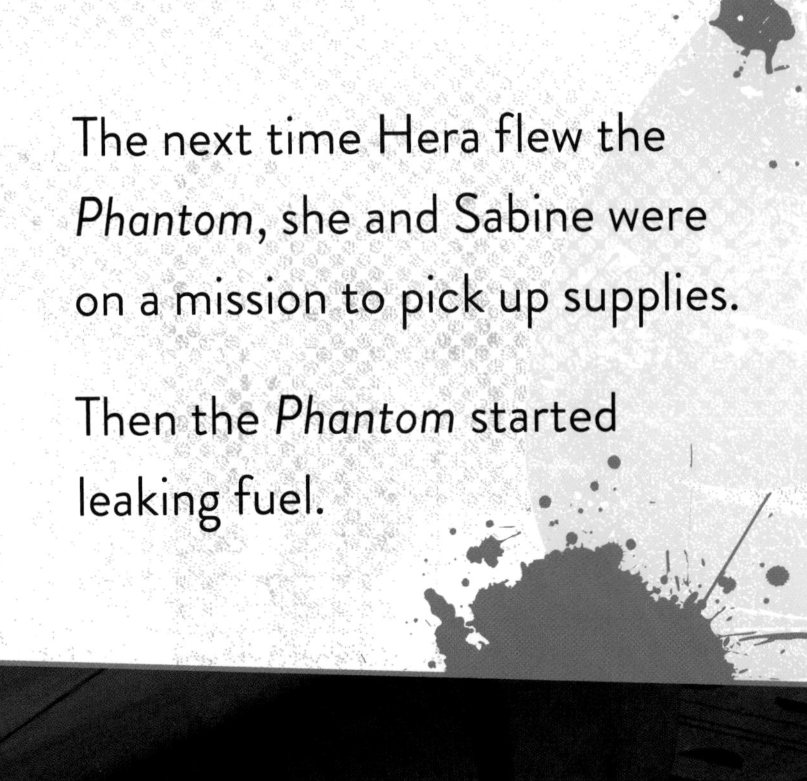

They put the supply boxes into the *Phantom*.

But all the fuel leaked out of the ship.

Without fuel, they were trapped!

They were also not alone.

Hera heard a noise from the shadows.

She saw a pair of glowing eyes.

Soon there were many glowing eyes.

There were monsters watching them!

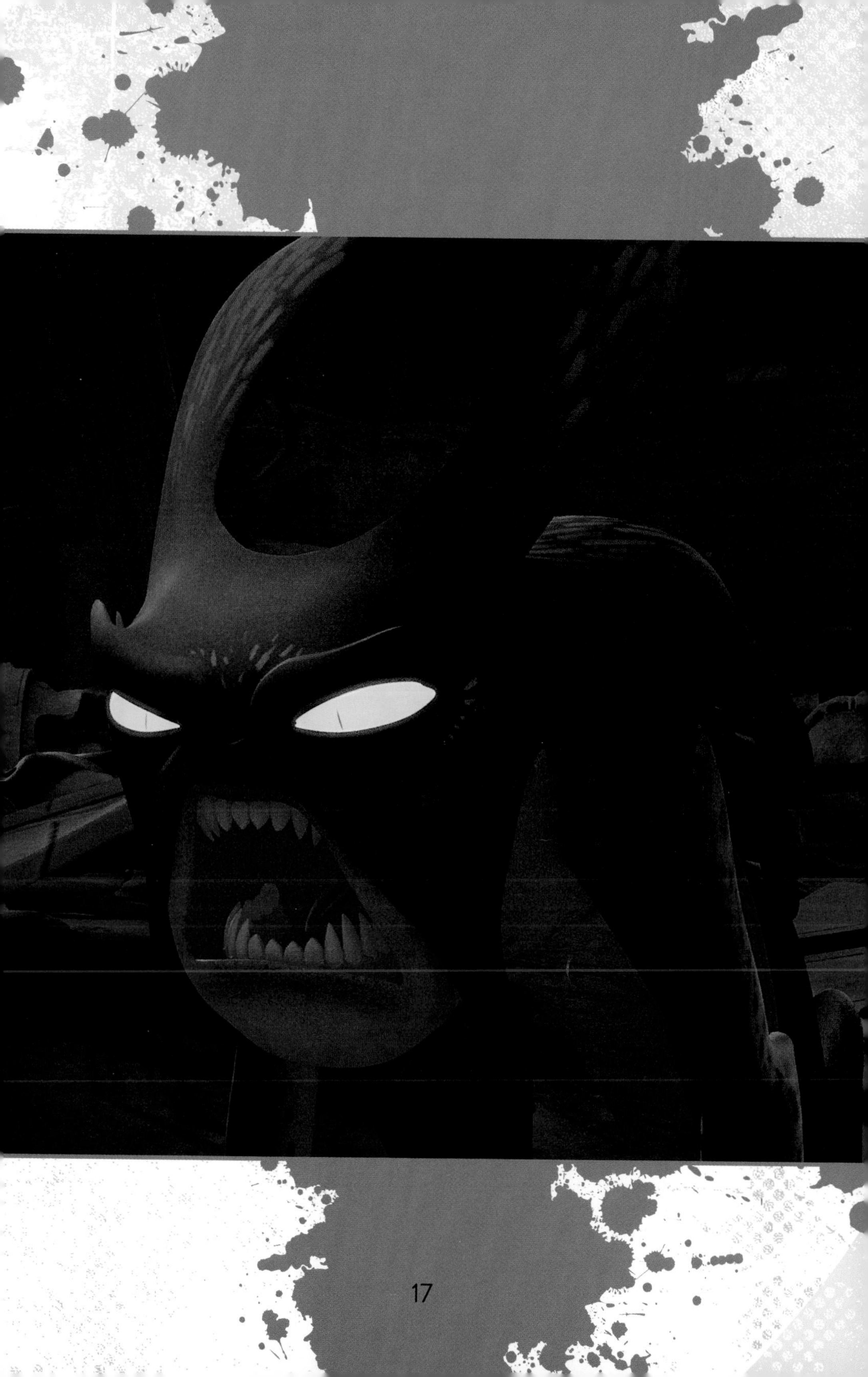

The monsters were called fyrnocks.

The fyrnocks had scary spikes on their faces, sharp claws, and pointy fangs.

Hera called the *Ghost* for help.

But the *Ghost* was far away.

It would take a while for the rebels to arrive.

Hera and Sabine would have to fight the fyrnocks.

Sabine had a plan.

They rolled big barrels between the monsters and the *Phantom*.

The barrels were full of a liquid that made things explode.

When the monsters came toward them, Hera would shoot the barrels.

Hera and Sabine heard a growl.

The monsters were coming.

Hera slowly aimed at the barrel closest to the monsters.

BOOM! The barrel blew up and took down a few monsters.

Hera fired at another barrel.

BOOM!

More monsters blew up.

BOOM! BOOM! BOOM!

Hera and Sabine blew up more barrels and more monsters.

But when they blew up the last barrel, there were still monsters left.

Hera and Sabine climbed on top of the *Phantom*.

They didn't know what to do next!

Then the *Ghost* arrived!

It flew close to the Phantom.

Hera and Sabine jumped on board.

They were safe!

But something was wrong.

Kanan couldn't get the *Ghost* to take off.

The monsters attacked the *Ghost*!

Hera took control and ran power through the ship's outside walls.

The power shocked the monsters!

“I didn’t know the *Ghost* could do that,” Kanan said.

“There’s a lot you don’t know about *my* ship,” Hera said.

Hera told Chopper how to fix the *Ghost*.

Then she flew above the *Phantom*.

Hera used the *Ghost*'s magnet lock to pick up the little ship.

Now everyone was safe.

Hera flew far, far away from the monsters.

Hera's fast flying saved the day!

The rebels are lucky to have a pilot like Hera.